NOISE AND SOUND

Lee-Anne Spalding

Bethany, Missouri

CONSTRUCTION SITE NOISE

There is a great deal of **noise** on a construction site! The noise or sound comes from many **sources**. Machines, tools, and people make noise.

MAKING AND HEARING NOISE

Sound Waves

Noise or sound is made when something **vibrates**. This vibration makes sound waves that travel through the air to our ears. Have you ever heard the sounds that a dump truck makes?

SOFT SOUNDS

The opposite of loud is quiet or soft. Some sounds on a construction site are soft. A handsaw makes a soft sound.

Trowel

Finishers are workers that put the finishing touches on buildings. They use a **trowel** that makes soft, scraping sounds.

HIGH SOUNDS

Some tools make high **pitched**, loud sounds. A circular saw makes a screeching sound that can hurt your ears!

For safety, big machines make beeping sounds when they back up. The workers hear the high pitched, loud beeps and know to move out of the way!

HELPFUL NOISE

Some noise is helpful on a construction site. To get the job done, workers must make noise by talking with fellow workers. Construction workers use walkie-talkies and cell phones to **communicate** with one another.

21

INDEX

FURTHER READING

Hudson, Cheryl W. *Construction Zone.* Candlewick Press, 2006.
Kilby, Don. *At a Construction Site.* Kids Can Press, 2006.

WEBSITES TO VISIT

Because Internet links change so often, Fitzgerald Books has developed an online list of websites related to the subject of this book. This site is updated regularly. Please use this link to access the list: www.fitzgeraldbookslinks.com/czs/ns

ABOUT THE AUTHOR

Lee-Anne Trimble Spalding is a former public school educator and is currently instructing preservice teachers at the University of Central Florida. She lives in Oviedo, Florida with her husband, Brett, and two sons, Graham and Gavin.